BGJ 11/9/15

THE AMAZING ADVENTURES OF SUPERMAN! ™

Magic Monsters!

by **Benjamin Bird**

illustrated by **Tim Levins**

Superman created by Jerry Siegel and Joe Shuster
by special arrangement with the Jerry Siegel family

PICTURE WINDOW BOOKS
a capstone imprint

The Amazing Adventures of Superman
is published by Picture Window Books
a Capstone Imprint
1710 Roe Crest Drive
North Mankato, Minnesota 56003
www.capstonepub.com

STAR34623

Cataloging-in-Publication Data is available at the Library of Congress website.
ISBN: 978-1-4795-6521-4 (library binding)
ISBN: 978-1-4795-6525-2 (paperback)
ISBN: 978-1-4795-8461-1 (eBook)

Summary: SUPERMAN and SHAZAM may have met their match when
Mister Mxyzptlk makes trouble in Metropolis. Will the daring duo be able to
stop the imp's . . . Magic Monsters?

Designer: Bob Lentz

Printed in the United States of America in North Mankato, Minnesota.
042015   008823CGF15

TABLE OF CONTENTS

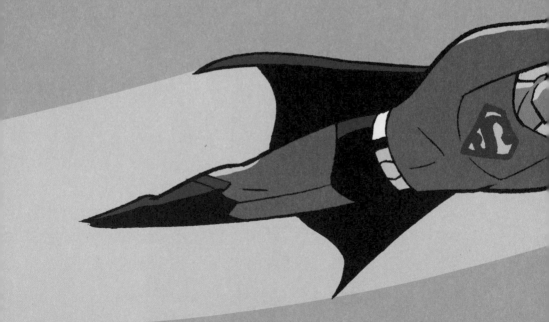

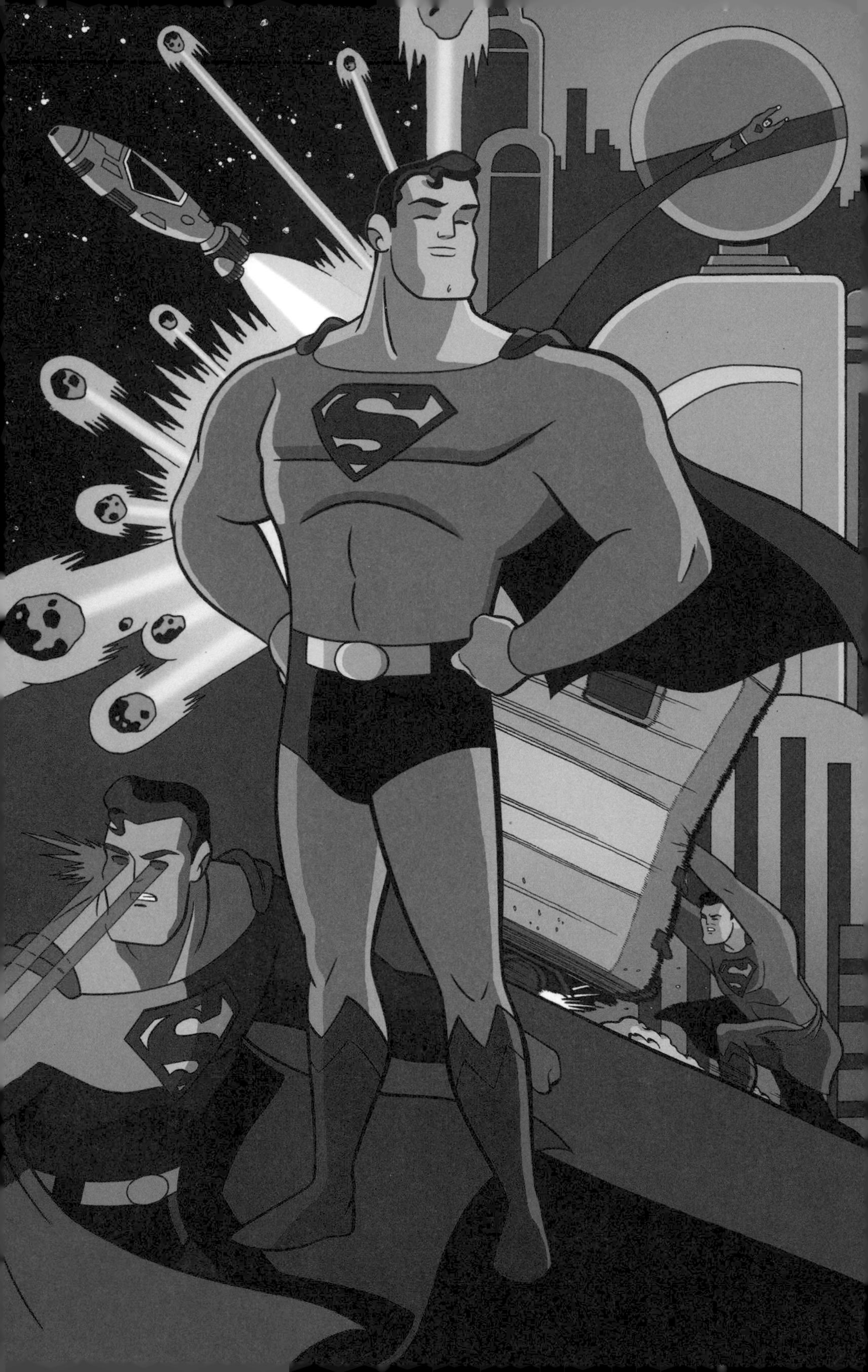

Born among the stars.
Raised on planet Earth.
With incredible powers,
he became the
World's Greatest Super Hero.
These are...

THE AMAZING ADVENTURES OF SUPERMAN!™

Chapter 1

EXTREME WEATHER

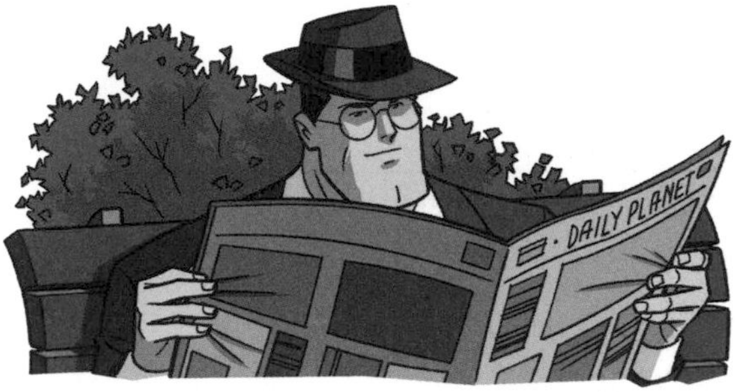
DAILY PLANET

Reporter Clark Kent sits on a bench in Metropolis. He opens a newspaper to a story he wrote. Seeing his name next to the headline always makes him smile.

Suddenly a shadow blocks
the sun. **FWOOSH!** A breeze
blows the paper from his
hands. Another gust rips his
hat from his head.

"Huh?" Clark says, looking up at the sky.

Above him, a green dragon flaps a pair of scaly wings. A fireball explodes from its jaws. **WHOOSH!**

Flames scorch Clark's suit and tie as he dives for cover.

Clark ducks into a nearby alley. He quickly removes his clothes. A red and blue uniform hides beneath.

ZOOM!

The super hero soars into the sky with a new identity and a new name. He is Superman!

Chapter 2

MASTERS OF MAGIC

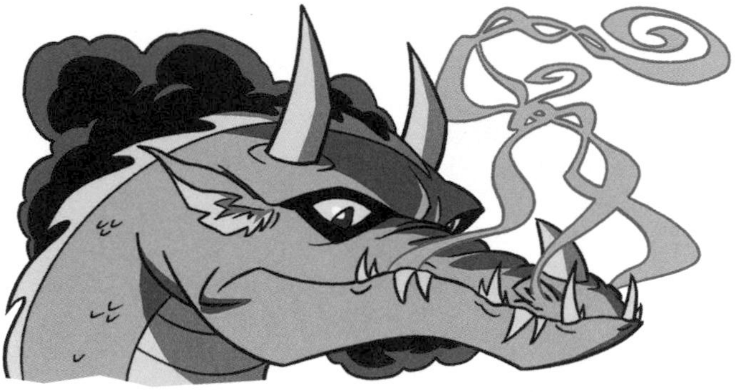

Smoke from the dragon's nostrils blackens the sky.

Superman fans the air in front of him. "Talk about dragon breath!" he jokes.

"Tee hee!" came a squeaky little laugh.

The Man of Steel turns toward the voice. A tiny man in a purple hat and suit floats near his shoulder.

"Mister Mxyzptlk!" says Superman. "What brings you here from the 5th Dimension?"

The magical imp laughs again. "I'm here to annoy you, as usual!" Mxy replies.

"It'll take more than a bird-brained dragon to ruffle my feathers," the super hero says.

"Well, my next guest is
sure to drive you up a wall,"
says Mxy. "Or INTO one!"

YOINK! A giant-sized

hand snatches Superman

from the sky.

The hand flings the

super hero into the wall of a

nearby building. **SMAAASH!**

Superman rises from the

rubble. "Two on one?" he

says. "I still like those odds."

Superman grabs a stone.

He throws it with his super-

strength. The rock strikes

the monster in its one eye.

The beast falls to the

ground with a **THUD!**

Then a third monster

appears! The creature

slithers on eight tentacles

toward a nearby boy.

The boy looks up and

cries out, **"SHAZAM!"**

KRA-KOOM! A bolt of lightning bursts from the sky and strikes the boy.

The child becomes the World's Mightiest Mortal, the super hero Shazam!

Chapter 3

THE NAME GAME

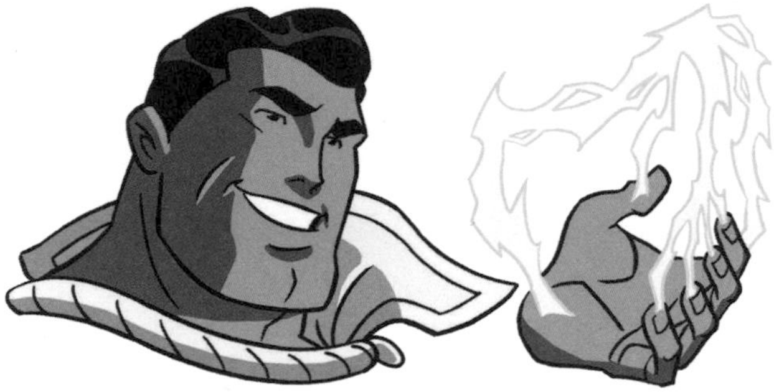

"I thought you could use my magic touch," Shazam tells Superman.

The super hero blasts electricity from his palms. It strikes the tentacled beast.

The monster falls but quickly rises. All three beasts attack the heroes.

Superman knows there is only one way to stop Mxy, once and for all.

"We must trick Mxy into saying his name backward," Superman tells his friend.

Shazam has a plan. "What do you call these monsters?" he asks Mxy.

"I haven't given them names," says Mxy, curious.

"Why not?" Shazam asks. "Names are powerful things, as we both know."

"You're right!" says Mxy. He points to the dragon. "I'll call this one Blaze."

Shazam points at the one-eyed giant. "Let's call this one Goliath," he says.

"My turn!" Superman

exclaims. He turns to the

strange creature with eight

tentacles. "And this last

one should be named . . .

Kltpzyxm!"

Mxy scratches his head and asks, "What kind of name is Kltpzyxm —?" **POOF!** Before he can finish, the imp vanishes back to the 5th Dimension.

A moment later, Mxy's magical monsters suddenly disappear too.

"Thanks for another amazing adventure!" Superman tells his friend.

Shazam smiles. "If there's ever anything else you need help with," he says, "just name it!"

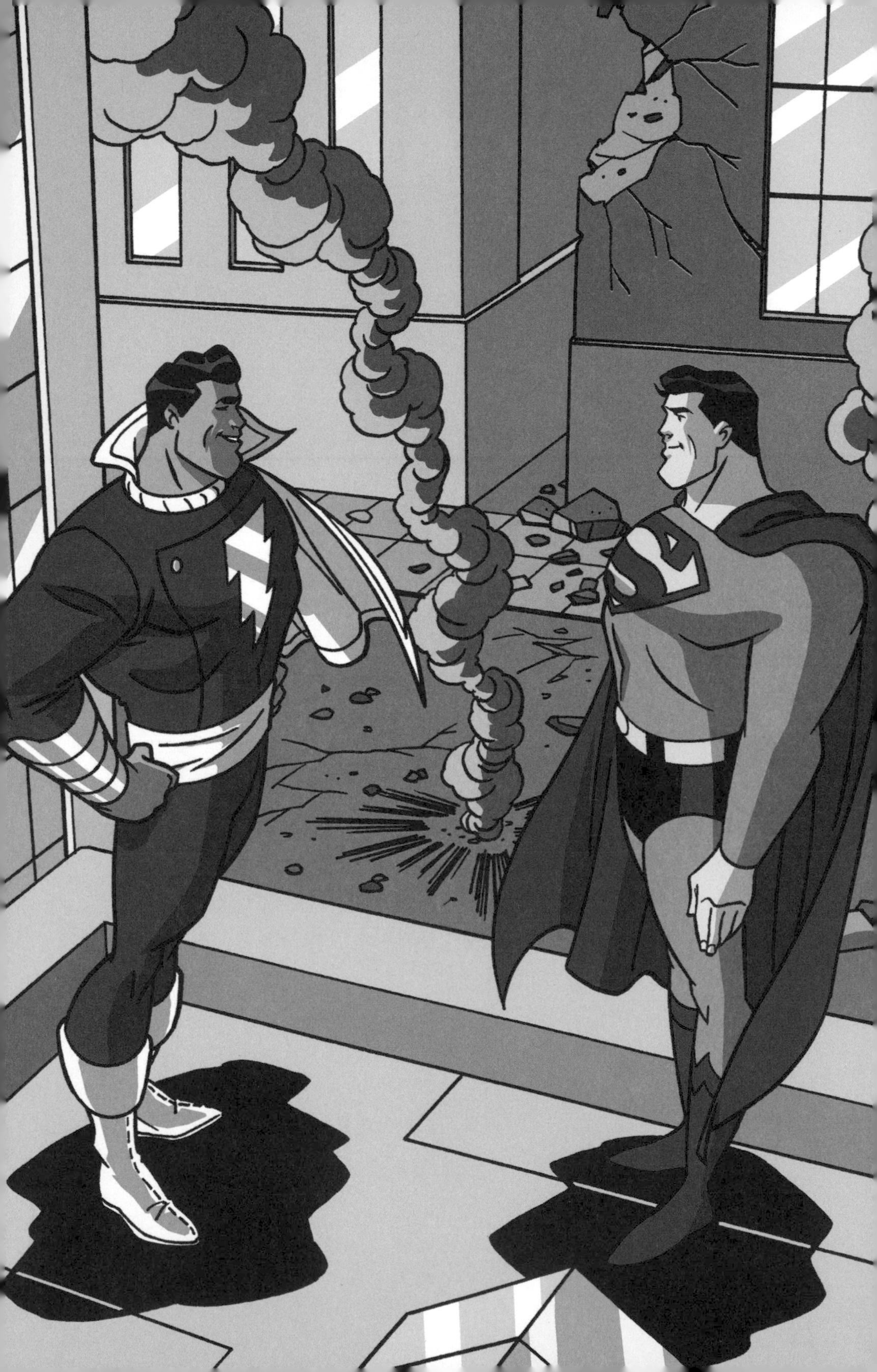

SUPERMAN'S SECRET MESSAGE!

Hey, kids! What super hero is known as the World's Mightiest Mortal?

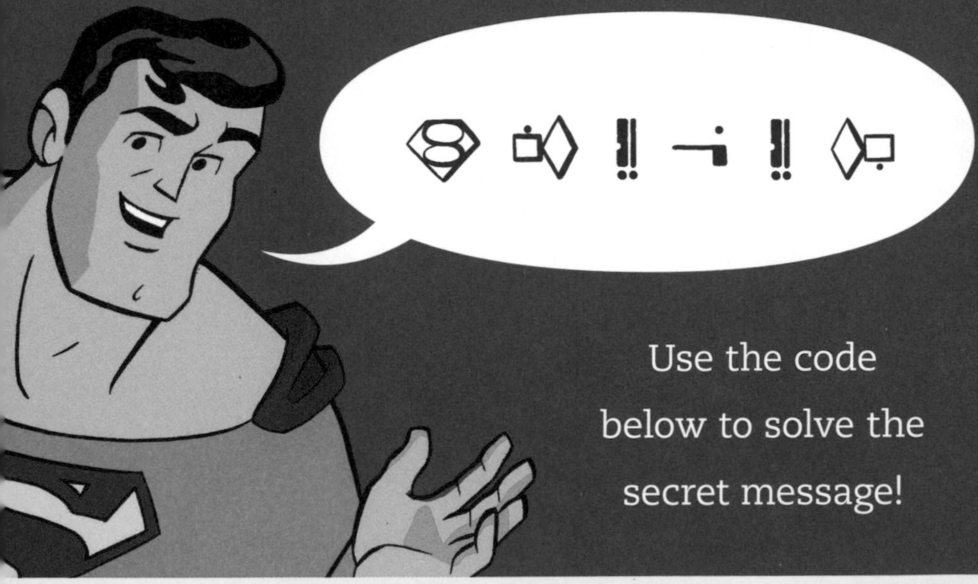

Use the code below to solve the secret message!

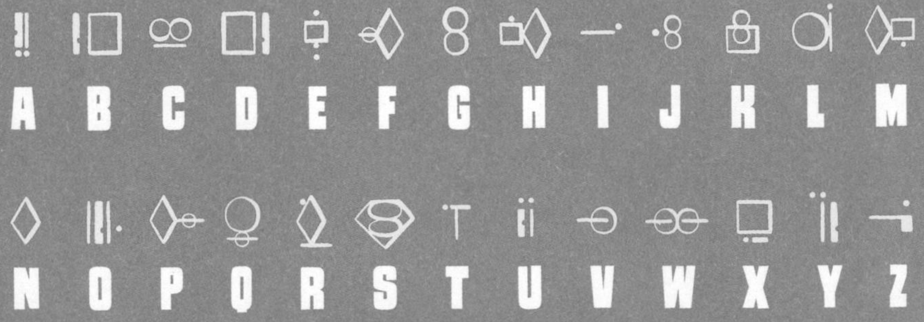
A B C D E F G H I J K L M
N O P Q R S T U V W X Y Z

nostrils (NOSS-truhlz) — the two openings in one's nose through which they breathe and smell

reporter (ri-POR-tur) — someone who gathers and reports the news

rubble (RUHB-uhl) — broken bricks and stones

tentacles (TEN0-tuh-kuhlz) — the long, flexible limbs of some animals, such as an octopus or squid

uniform (YOO-nuh-form) — a special set of clothes worn by a super hero

villain (VIL-uhn) — an evil person

THE AMAZING ADVENTURES OF SUPERMAN!™

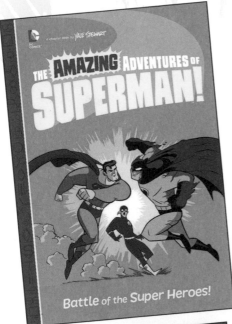

DC COMICS
a chapter book by YALE STEWART
THE AMAZING ADVENTURES OF SUPERMAN!
Battle of the Super Heroes!

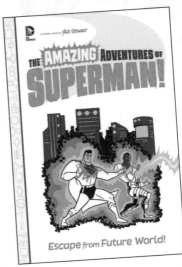

DC COMICS
a chapter book by YALE STEWART
THE AMAZING ADVENTURES OF SUPERMAN!
Escape from Future World!

DC COMICS
a chapter book by YALE STEWART
THE AMAZING ADVENTURES OF SUPERMAN!
Alien Superman!

DC COMICS
a chapter book by YALE STEWART
THE AMAZING ADVENTURES OF SUPERMAN!
Creatures from Planet X!

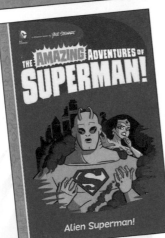

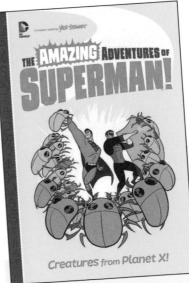

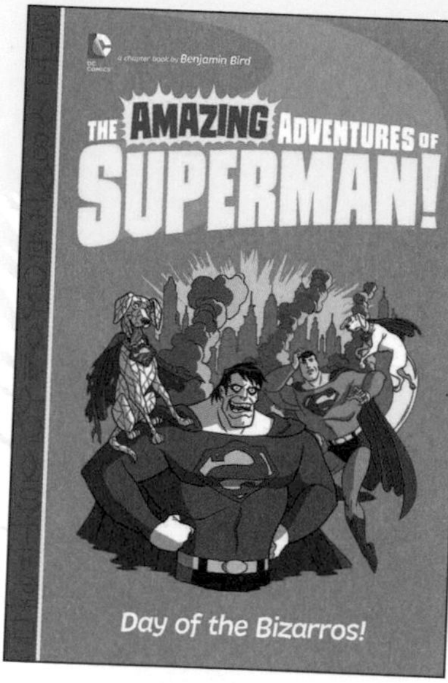
a chapter book by Benjamin Bird
THE AMAZING ADVENTURES OF SUPERMAN!
Day of the Bizarros!

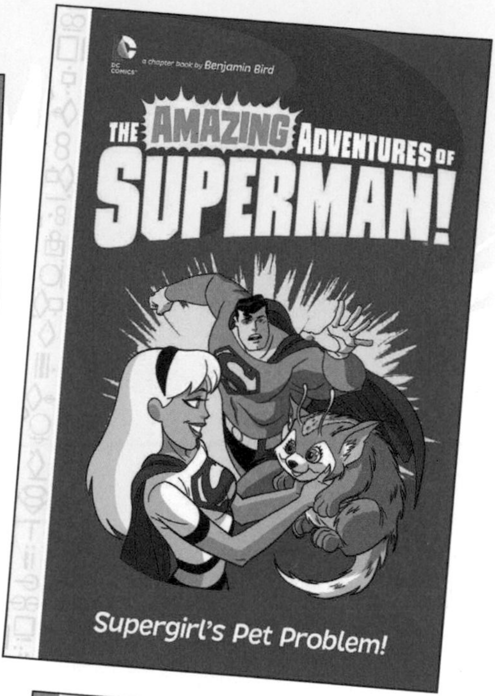
DC COMICS
a chapter book by Benjamin Bird
THE AMAZING ADVENTURES OF SUPERMAN!
Supergirl's Pet Problem!

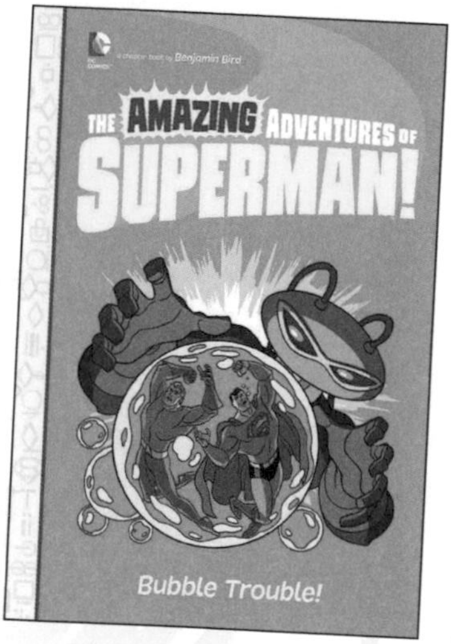
a chapter book by Benjamin Bird
THE AMAZING ADVENTURES OF SUPERMAN!
Bubble Trouble!

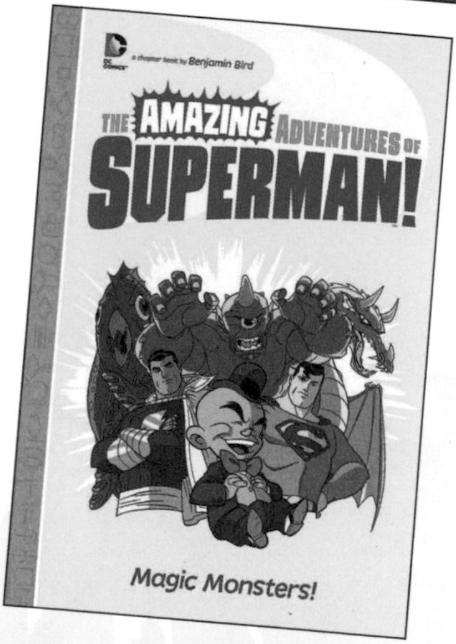
a chapter book by Benjamin Bird
THE AMAZING ADVENTURES OF SUPERMAN!
Magic Monsters!

COLLECT THEM ALL!

only from . . . **PICTURE WINDOW BOOKS**

Author

Benjamin Bird is a children's book editor and writer from St. Paul, Minnesota. He has written books about some of today's most popular characters, including Batman, Superman, Wonder Woman, Scooby-Doo, Tom & Jerry, and more.

Illustrator

Tim Levins is best known for his work on the Eisner Award-winning DC Comics series Batman: Gotham Adventures. Tim has illustrated other DC titles, such as Justice League Adventures and Batgirl. He enjoys life in Midland, Ontario, Canada, with his wife, son, dog, and two horses.